Love and Love

Jon Peirce

i

For Ingrid McCarthy, who encouraged me to break into electronic self-publishing, and to the as yet unknown Ms. Right. I should also like to acknowledge the fine book cover design work done by Andre Malard.

Love and Love

Once upon a time, a long, long time ago, when Ike ruled the U.S. with soothing, banal nostrums, instant mashed potatoes were all the rage, and any car worth its salt had big tail fins, there was an eighth-grade boy named Fred Dawson. Fred was neither more nor less awkward than average for a boy his age, which meant exceptionally awkward, particularly around girls and above all around girls whom he wished to impress. His 6', 190-lb. frame somehow made his awkwardness seem worse, at least to him.

Fred attended Shoshone Junior High School in Westport, Connecticut. So did a raven-haired Italian girl named Gloria Cavalieri, who was in the ninth grade. Of average height, Gloria had sparkling black eyes and an incredible energy, which came from her ability to focus completely on whatever it was she happened to be doing at that time. At the moment when this story begins, Gloria's main focus was on her tennis game.

Both she and Fred were alums of Shoshone's summer tennis program, more familiarly known as the Shoshone School of Athletic Self-Help. Whatever anyone had managed to learn about the game was in no way due to the efforts of the instructor, a large, horsy woman from the Philadelphia Main Line—could her name really have been Bev MacWhinney--who, after teaching the assembled group the barest rudiments during the first two sessions, spent the rest of the summer sitting in the official's chair drinking coffee from a large Thermos and reading the *New York Times*. But there may have been a bit of method to Bev's madness after all; at least she let people play, and therefore did not actively turn off anyone who was really interested. Gloria was definitely in this category. So, too, was Fred, especially after discovering that Gloria was. But during the summer program, he'd been too shy to ask her to play, what with all the ninth-grade guys hanging around her, most of them more handsome and far more self-confident than he. To his surprise and delight, though, she kept on playing during the following school year.

During that year, Gloria somehow managed to get in a game almost every day, during school hours—and almost always with a different boy. Like Catherine the Great, whose appetite for the opposite sex was allegedly totally insatiable, so did Gloria appear to have an insatiable appetite for different male tennis partners. Only once, in fact, did Fred see her playing with another girl, and on that occasion, it was clear she wasn't enjoying the game one bit.

She soon became a familiar sight, tossing her black braids in perfect rhythm with the ball as she served. Her breasts were small but well-defined; her hips could have launched, well, at least seven or eight hundred ships. It wasn't long before the sight of those whirling braids, flashing black eyes and swaying hips was enough to turn Fred on mightily.

For several months in the early fall and then again in the spring, he suffered in silence. Then, finally, one warm May day, he got up the courage to ask Gloria if she would play with him after school. To his immense surprise, she accepted.

"There's just one thing," she said. "We need to play during school hours. I've got a job every day after school. Don't you have a study hall seventh period?"

"Yes, but I'm supposed to be there. How can I get out of it?"

"Oh, my dad can arrange that quite easily," she laughed. It was then that he remembered that her father was assistant principal in charge of discipline and scheduling, which no doubt explained why she hadn't been seen in *her* seventh period study hall since early April, except on the rainiest of days. Thinking that this represented a rather blatant flaunting of her official connections, Fred nonetheless applied to Mr. Cavalieri for an exemption from the next day's study hall, an exemption that was quickly granted.

"As I remember, you had straight 'A's' in all your academic subjects, but only a 'C' in Phys. Ed. So this is giving you extra work where you need it most," laughed Cavalieri, a stocky, genial sort somewhat below average height. For his part, Fred was amazed at the man's sheer powers of recall.

The pair met at the tennis court, a makeshift facility which had been put smack in the middle of the school's parking lot, then enclosed in a high wire fence, on the stroke of two the next afternoon. At this stage, Fred's tennis game consisted mainly of a booming serve which went in 20% of the time on a good day, and an equally powerful forehand drive with an accuracy rate around 50%. Backhands were always an adventure, and as for volleying, well, that was for volleyball. He wondered how Gloria would respond to the powerful but crude and very limited tools in his arsenal.

What struck him right away, that first time they played, was how long she took to warm up. For him, the warm-up was mainly a social obligation, something to be got through as soon as possible so you could get on with the game. It had been rare, in his previous experience, for a warm-up to last longer than five minutes; many had been even shorter. With Gloria, twenty minutes wasn't enough. After trading a huge assortment of forehands, backhands, and volleys with Fred—even a lob and a smash or two—she still wasn't ready so much as to practice her serve. Finally, after another ten minutes of long, searching rallies from the baseline, she was ready. The two went up to the net, where she spun her racket. The letter they called came down 'W' instead of 'M,' which meant she served.

After a dozen or so practice serves apiece, the game itself was finally underway. Though Fred had been concerned at how long the warm-up was waking, especially since he knew Gloria had to leave shortly after 3 to be at her job on time, he had to admit that it made a difference to the type of game they were playing. With his muscles thoroughly warmed-up and hand-eye coordination improved, Fred found that it was no longer a case of do or die on each shot. He was able to keep the ball in play much better than in the past, and by the end of the third game, the two were starting to have some long, occasionally exciting rallies.

Though Gloria rarely hit the ball very hard--certainly nowhere near as hard as her bigger, stronger male opponent--she managed to get to most of his shots. The rhythm of her game was smooth and fluid. After a while, a bit of this rubbed off on him. Instead of trying to knock the bejesus out of the ball or put it in a totally unreachable place every time, he would, every now and then, hit it in such a way that the rally would continue. To be sure, the old killer instinct would surface every now and then, in the shape of a monstrous cross-court forehand—raising a smile from Gloria—but within half an hour, the two were sometimes having rallies of 10 to 20 shots, something Fred had never before experienced in a tennis match.

All too soon, it was time for her to leave and head off to her job as clerk in a local grocery store. The two had managed to finish only six games, splitting them evenly, but Fred felt as if he had learned more about the fundamental nature of the game than he had from his previous hundred matches *in toto*. A certain sadness came over him as he walked with Gloria to the bike racks; he felt as if he were pulling away in the middle of something very beautiful. But this feeling was quickly dissipated by

Gloria's friendly, yet challenging words. "So when are we going to play again? We're not going to leave it like this, are we?"

"Oh, definitely not! Whenever you want—so long as your dad can keep letting me out of study hall."

"Let me tell you a secret. He'll always be glad to let you out of study hall. It's like this. He was getting a bit concerned about some of the guys I was playing with before. The leather jacket set, you know. Thought they weren't, how shall I put it, the right social element for the daughter of a professional."

"I didn't know those guys were interested in tennis."

"Well, most of them really weren't. It was me they were interested in—and their level of play showed it. Anyway, about the game. Is next Tuesday at 2 OK?"

"Perfect. Do I need to go see your dad, or can he send a note?"

"Let's see if he'll send a note. Bye-bye."

Sure enough, the next Tuesday morning Fred's homeroom teacher handed him a typed envelope bearing the name of the study hall supervisor. "I don't know what's going on here," the homeroom teacher said with a shrug, "but as long as you keep on getting 'A's' I guess I'm not going to worry about it too much." With a sheepish grin, Fred crammed the envelope into his book bag. He was at that precise stage of early adolescence where good grades could be more of a social liability than an asset, at least in front of other boys.

At five to two, Fred went to the washroom, changed into his tennis whites, and raced out to the parking lot to meet Gloria. She was already there, slowly but methodically banging a ball against the wall to practice her ground strokes. It was clear that she'd been looking forward to the match. As soon as she saw Fred coming, her face lit up and she became more animated in all her movements and gestures.

"If you thought last week was good, just wait till you see what I can do today," she said.

"I'm ready for you," Fred replied, hoping he'd managed to cover up some lingering traces of fear with this bluff note of masculine determination.

This time, the warm-up was even longer and more searching than it had been the week before. It started at mid-court, with the gentlest taps back and forth just to establish a rhythm. Then it moved to the backline, where the pair had several dozen long, searching exchanges of ground strokes. Both took the net, and they even took turns hitting each other lobs to smash back.

Fred was enjoying all of this immensely, but he was also concerned that the extremely long warm-up—which was by no means finished at 2:30—would leave them little if any time to play.

"We don't have to worry about that," Gloria said expansively when Fred finally mentioned the time.

"Why not? I thought you had a job to go to."

"Oh, I guess I didn't tell you. The store agreed to give me Tuesdays off on condition I work two hours longer on Saturday. This afternoon is *ours,* my friend."

"Let's make the most of it, then," said Fred, starting a rally which culminated in a huge cross-court forehand that Gloria somehow managed to tap back, just over the net, and just out of the reach of his thrusting racket.

"Time to start serving," Gloria said. Each tried about three dozen serves, taking them from a variety of different angles and heights. Gloria won the toss again. Then the two shook hands and the game was on.

"Let's see. We were at three-all last time. Shall we finish the old set up before starting a new one?"

"Whatever you want," Fred replied gallantly.

"I like to finish what I start," she said, tossing the ball up high in her usual, leisurely way, and somehow making sure that her black braids got tossed at the same time.

(Fred hadn't yet learned how to keep the flying braids from distracting his attention from the game). Her first serve of the game had just the slightest bit of spin on it—something Fred hadn't seen much of before. Whether because of the unaccustomed spin or the sight of the flying braids, he was just a bit too early with his powerful forehand return, and drove the ball into the top of the net. "Fifteen-love," she sang out. Her next serve was harder, but also flatter. This time Fred pasted his return into his opponent's backhand corner for an outright winner.

Gloria won the first game rather easily; then Fred's big serve allowed him to even the score. In Gloria's second service game, with the two more fully warmed up and used to each other, the rallies started to become longer and more interesting. Fred even put up one of the high lobs he was just beginning to use. While Gloria was able to handle it, it was clearly a challenge for her, as she tapped a slow return that he was easily able to put away. Fred resolved to try the shot again before too long. But before he had fully registered that thought, Gloria had sent in another spin service, this time to his backhand. The spin made the ball take an unexpectedly high bounce, winding up around Fred's chest. Unprepared for the bounce, he could do no better than chop at the ball weakly, sending it to about mid-court. Gloria, who *was* prepared, sent a crisp forehand into Fred's backhand corner, running to the net as she did so. Fred made a valiant effort to retrieve the ball, but was unable to do more than put it into the net. Advantage Cavalieri.

Serving for the game, Gloria placed a medium-speed serve right on the center line—a shot which she had learned was usually a winner. But this time, Fred was ready. Drawing back his right arm, he sent a huge forehand deep into the corner on Gloria's backhand side. Barely managing to get her racket on the shot, she sent a half-lob back to about halfway between mid-court and the back line. He debated smashing the ball, but decided the bounce wasn't quite high enough, and instead put up his own lob— a higher and deeper one that landed near the corner on Gloria's forehand side. She responded with a pretty good, deep lob of her own, and for what seemed an eternity the two exchanged these gentle, airborne missiles. "A game of nerves," Fred thought to himself, as he handled the eighth or ninth shot in the series. This lob went deep into the corner, and Gloria was barely able to return it, just tapping the ball over the net. Exercising masterful restraint at a time when he was tempted to crush the ball, he simply flicked it a few feet over the net, leaving Gloria flat-footed at the back line. Deuce, yet again.

A third spin serve from Gloria fooled Fred yet again; trying to add a bit of his own spin simply caused him to chop the ball into the net. Her next serve was flatter, and Fred put a hard forehand down the line for an outright winner. Then she went back to the center-stripe serve again. Fred was able to return it, but only just barely. With her own forehand, not big but surprisingly sure and accurate, Gloria put the ball into Fred's backhand corner. Somehow he caught up to it, but again was able to hit only a weak return. Standing at the net by now, Gloria put the ball away easily. Advantage Cavalieri.

Now she tried to put the game away with yet another spin serve. This time, Fred took a different approach, realizing that hitting the ball too hard would only be self-defeating. Instead, he flicked a short backhand to a point about halfway between the net and mid-court. Caught flat-footed at the back line, Gloria could do no more than wave her hands and say "Good shot. Where did you learn that one, anyway?"

"I have my sources," Fred said mysteriously. Truth to tell, he'd seen her experimenting with the shot in the pre-game warm-up and had decided to try it out himself. But he wasn't about to tell *her* that.

"I'll get you for that!" she said.

"Go ahead and try!" he replied. "I'll be ready for you." He liked the flash in her eyes as they bantered. Hypnotic, he thought. But before he could get too comfortable with his fantasies, she'd put the next serve right at his feet. Without breaking stride, he kept the rally going with the old "ice-cream scoop" shot he'd honed at the School of Self-Help. The shot entailed lifting the ball off the ground with a sickle-like motion and flipping it right back at his opponent. Now it was Gloria who was caught off-balance, as the ball landed at her feet. She attempted her own version of the same shot, but it wasn't a move she was familiar with, so her return went high and deep. Advantage Dawson.

Once again, Gloria's black eyes flashed. When she served, she flipped her braids so hard that they went straight up in the air behind her. This caught Fred just enough off-balance that his backhand return of her center-stripe serve went six inches wide. Another deuce.

For her next serve, she went back to the spin that had won her points earlier in the game. Fred was ready with another of his short, quick backhand flicks, but this time

Gloria was ready, too, and volleyed the ball back before it had hit the ground. Now the two exchanged short, searching volleys. It was a real test of hand-eye coordination, an area in which Fred was (secretly at least) prepared to admit his opponent probably had the edge. Displaying what was for him remarkable patience, Fred stayed within his game, not attempting to do more than match Gloria's strength for a dozen or more exchanges. Finally he found a soft backhand volley to his forehand just a bit too tempting. Shifting his grip, he put just enough spin on his return to make the shot unreturnable, even if she caught up with it. But that was also just enough spin to make the shot go an inch and a half wide in the doubles alley. Advantage Cavalieri.

After this amazing rally, the next point was anti-climactic. Gloria hit an ordinary flat serve just a little harder than usual, and Fred foolishly tried adding his own power to the shot instead of simply meeting the ball. His return sailed 15 feet out. Five-four for Cavalieri.

"Don't get mad, get even," Fred told himself. Over the next minute and a half, he did just that, booming unreturnable serves down the center-stripe, crunching massive forehands to the corner when Gloria did manage to return his serves, and even making a fine shot at the net, where he rarely played in singles. Now the score was 5-all, and the time was ten past four.

"Shall we call this one a tie and move on to the new set?" Fred was surprised to hear Gloria asking as they walked to mid-court for a much-needed drink of water.

"Sure—but I thought you were the one who liked to finish what you started," Fred said.

"I—well, I'm not sure we're ever going to finish this one," Gloria replied.

"If you ask me, I think a tie a very fitting result for the kind of game we had," Fred said gallantly. "Shall we spin again for serve in the new set?"

Fred spun his racket, and once again Gloria won the serve. Incorporating just about everything they'd learned from the pre-game and the completion of the old set, the pair kept at it for nearly two hours. The score was 8-all, and neither player showed any signs of yielding. "I'd love to keep on with this until the sky was pitch black," Fred finally said. "Unfortunately, it's my turn to cook dinner tonight. If I don't show up to do that, I'll be grounded."

Gloria's magnificent eyes flashed again. This time, some sympathy and understanding were mixed in with the earlier note of challenge. "So they trust boys in your house to do the cooking, do they?" she said, secretly impressed.

"If you like to eat, you can learn to cook," Fred replied. "Both my parents work, so the skill comes in handy every now and then. And I don't have any sisters (or brothers, either), so if a relief cook is needed, it's going to be me. Besides, it beats washing dishes. On the nights when I cook, I don't have to touch a single dish."

"That's only fair," said Gloria. "Well, I'll be seeing you again next week. Shall we start a new set or finish up this one?"

"Let's start a brand new set," suggested Fred. "That is, if you're ready to call this one a tie."

The two shook on that, and Fred was pleasantly surprised to feel Gloria squeezing his hand and twisting his thumb, as he did hers.

"See you later, alligator!" he called her to her as he got on his bike for the ride home.

"After a while, crocodile," she laughed, as she got on hers.

Fred's ride home took longer than usual because of his huge erection, which wouldn't go down even when he tried to tame it by thinking about the previous week's Episcopal church sermon. He was glad he'd had the foresight to cover up his shorts with his sweater while saying goodbye to Gloria, and also that his parents weren't home to see him walking in the door still fully rampant.

Their tennis games continued in much the same vein throughout the spring. As they grew more used to playing with each other, the rallies and, in consequence, the games and sets became longer and longer. It was not uncommon for their matches to last until 6:30, or even sometimes past 7:00, Fred having had the foresight to get excused from cooking duties on Tuesdays. Their last meeting of the school year went until 7:45. Though the match itself had lasted well over four hours, Gloria and Fred had played just two sets (14-12 for her, 11-9 for him). As they staggered off the court, Fred felt an equal mixture of exhaustion, exhilaration, and plain old randiness. At his suggestion, they stopped at the nearby drugstore for a 7-Up on the way home. Given the lateness of the hour, however, both felt it wise not to linger over the drink.

Come summer, the two were able to play more frequent if shorter matches. It got so they would play two or three evenings a week if weather permitted. Then, in early July, came the news he had been dreading. Phillips Exeter Academy (aka Exeter) had taken Fred off the wait list and admitted him. He had no idea why he was being sent away to boarding school. After all, it wasn't as if

Westport had a bad system or his grades were bad and he needed more motivation to study. The town had some of the best teachers (and highest teacher salaries) in the country, and Fred was getting 'A's' in all his academic subjects. If anything, he was a bit too much of a grind. His parents had in fact sometimes complained that he always had his nose in a book and should be spending more time with other people his age. Why in hell would they then send him off to this virtual cloister?

The only reason he could think of for his being sent away to school was that his parents had both gone and thought it was the thing to do. When he protested that he didn't really want to go away and didn't feel he needed to, his father shushed him right away. "It's a done deal," he said. "You're going away to school in the fall. End of discussion." At this, Fred felt both frightened and completely unwanted.

For several days, he delayed communicating the news to Gloria. But after their next game she noticed that his complexion looked pale and that he was a lot less talkative than usual. "Is there something wrong?" she asked.

"Yes," he said. "As a matter of fact there is—something very wrong." Then he told her about being sent away to school.

"But that's terrible," she said. "Why go if you don't want to? I'm sure there are lots of other boys who would be really happy to take your place."

"That's what I told my dad, but he didn't listen to me. I really got the feeling he just wanted to get me out of the house. Sort of like last year's lawn furniture."

"How terrible!" Gloria said again. She put her arms around him and gave him a tight hug—the first ever in their acquaintanceship.

"Well, we've got nearly two more months," Fred said after the hug had ended. "Let's make the most of them."

Throughout the rest of the summer, they played with vigor and enthusiasm, an enthusiasm that sometimes bordered on desperation. The Saturday after Labor Day, they played their final match of the season. Fred would be going away to Exeter the next week. For some reason, Fred's shots lacked some of their usual authority, and his serve was also a bit off. Gloria won three straight sets rather easily—the first time this had ever happened.

"Of course, we'll keep in touch through the year," Fred said, as they shared a final 7-Up at the drugstore.

"Of course. And we'll play again next summer," Gloria said.

"Absolutely."

The two briefly embraced, tears streaming down both their cheeks as they did so. As Fred was getting on his bike, Gloria waved. But it was a sad, wistful wave instead of her usual peppy one. Fred didn't even have the heart to wave back. A week later, he was ensconced at Exeter, and finding himself having to carry seniors' heavy trunks up long, winding back staircases, all part of the wonderful ritual called prepping.

Gloria's weekly letters, warm and chatty and written in peacock-blue ink, were the only bright spot in what was otherwise a dreadful year. For the first time ever, Fred had difficulty with some of his courses, getting 'D' or 'F' in the fall term in everything except English, where he was fortunate enough to maintain a 'B+'. The food was terrible, the coat-and-tie requirement and 9:30 lights-out rule childish, and the required daily chapel services moronic. Worse still, he had great difficulty making friends, though by Christmas there were two or three other boys he could talk to. When he and Gloria met downtown over Christmas for a cup of coffee, she looked at him worriedly.

"You really don't look well," she said. "The place doesn't seem to agree with you at all. Can't you arrange to flunk out, or get kicked out?"

"I'd like to," he said. "But my dad would make my life a living hell if I did that. I'm afraid I'm going to have to tough it out if I possibly can." The topic of conversation quickly changed, but it was as if a cloud had come across the horizon on a beautiful summer day, and not left.

By spring vacation, Fred was feeling a bit more cheerful, but the improvement was marginal. His grades were up somewhat, and he had made a couple more friends. During the spring, he managed to improve his grades a good deal more, narrowly missing the honor roll for the spring trimester, and finished the year just above the middle of the class. He remained unhappy, though, both because he missed Gloria and because he found the ascetic, all-male social atmosphere sterile and boring. When he got home in early June, the first thing he did was ask his parents if he could withdraw, instead of going back for a second year. For the first time, he told them frankly about Gloria, and also said he was generally unhappy with the social life and not that happy with the academic life.

This time, they listened a bit more attentively. They talked back and forth for more than half an hour. Finally his father said. "Well, you've given it a good try. And I'm not really sure it does agree with you. So let's try this. You go back for one more term, and if you're still feeling unhappy at Christmas, we'll take you out and you can go to Staples High." Elated at this unexpected victory, Fred rushed to call Gloria and give her the good news, as well as setting up their first tennis match of the season. Even though by this time both knew of better courts, they chose to return to their old stomping grounds at the junior high.

Fred had only played a couple of times during the spring, and found himself pretty badly out of practice when compared to Gloria, who had kept up twice-weekly games (admittedly with lesser opponents) since April. Though he'd started to recover much of his form after an hour's rally, she still managed to beat him fairly easily in three straight sets. At Fred's suggestion, they rallied for an extra half hour after the match. He could see Gloria smiling approvingly near the end of this second rally session, as their exchanges became longer and more flowing. Clearly their old rhythm was coming back.

Before their next match, which they set for the following Tuesday afternoon (this still being Gloria's day off from the store), Fred spent several hours hitting balls against the school's high brick wall, and a couple more hours practicing his serve. On the appointed day, their pre-match rally was even more thorough and intense than usual, and the pre-game handshake bordered on ferocity. The flash in Gloria's eyes could have ignited paper. As for Fred, though his expression was calmer, his determination to win was equally apparent.

Gloria won the toss, and started off the match with a perfectly placed serve to Fred's backhand. But he'd worked on the stroke hard since their last match, and was able to send a hard cross-court return to his opponent's backhand. Now it was she who was forced to scramble, putting up a half-lob that landed just behind mid-court. For a change, his smash stayed in. Love-15, in favor of Dawson. He didn't keep the lead for long, though, as Gloria next spun a serve at his feet, and his slice return went into the net.

Each won his or her own serve rather easily, but then, as had usually been the case in the past, the match started to tighten up in the third game, with the two players warmed up and used to each other. Gloria was mixing up her serves as never before, keeping Fred continually off-balance. Moreover, she had over the past year added a good high lob to her arsenal of shots. Fred could usually handle this shot, but it kept him from charging the net when he might otherwise have done so and helped her put more shots away in the corners. At the same time, his big serve was working better than it usually did, and he was also scoring points with tricky short spin shots and a long, curving "sickle-hook" backhand, in addition to his usual crushing cross-court and down the line forehand and cross-court backhand. As a result, the games grew longer and longer, some running to 15 or even 20 deuces. An hour of hard play saw the two tied, 6-6. A half hour later, Fred finally managed to break Gloria's serve, thanks in large measure to his hardest forehand of the year and a spin shot that described a full semi-circle before landing just out of Gloria's reach. Then, though Gloria fought valiantly, Fred's booming serves were simply too much for her. First set to Dawson, 11-9.

No words were needed. After a short break for a rest and water, the two threw fierce glances at each other, as if to say that, long as it had been, the first set would be a cakewalk compared to the second one. Gloria threw down the gauntlet early on, breaking Fred's serve at game 1 with the help of a rare double fault on his part and two beautiful down-the-line forehands into the corner. He returned the favor at game 4, mixing up high lobs, net smashes, and cross-court forehands to good advantage. Fred held his serve relatively easily in the next game; then the two battled back and forth through 35 deuces before Gloria finally held her own serve. Game 7 was another see-saw affair, with Gloria hitting some of the best service returns Fred had ever seen. Eventually, she was rewarded with another service break—but only after 21 deuces.

In game 10, with Gloria serving for the set at 5-4, Fred hit the peak of his ground game, crushing her serves with a series of cross-court backhands as well as forehands and finishing off with a spectacular smash at the net. His play was so exceptional in this game that Gloria was moved to congratulate him. Each held their serve relatively easily; then the real battle began, with the score tied 6-6. (There was no such thing as a tie-breaker in those days). The next game had 19 deuces; the one after that, 25. Even the individual points were often long, as Fred was starting to hit more and more lobs as a way of conserving energy. Then, after two more relatively short games in which serve was held, Fred started off by hitting two straight double-faults, something he had not done since his first weeks of play. He fought valiantly through 14 deuces and some incredibly long points marked by sky-high lobs on both sides, but was never able to put Gloria away. After 20 minutes, she broke his serve with a short backhand flip that dropped just in front of his feet. Cavalieri serving for the set at 9-8.

The next game (number 18) was a virtual repeat of the one that had gone before it, except that Gloria didn't double-fault. She alternated devastating spin serves with flat ones down the line or in the backhand corner. While he managed a few outright winners, mostly from his forehand, he also hit his share of balls into the net or long. And there were a good many really long rallies, some involving over 40 exchanges. On the 15th deuce, his cross-court backhand return went just barely long. Then she managed to lob back his devastating forehand return of her center-stripe serve, starting a succession of a dozen or more lobs which ended only when he smashed one of hers a foot long. Second set to Cavalieri, 10-8.

Mere mortals would have broken off for the day at this point. After all, the two had been playing for three and a half hours, not including the pre-game warm-up, and the sun was much lower on the horizon than it had been. On this day, at least, Fred and Gloria were not mere mortals. So passionate and fierce was their rivalry that both would have died rather than adjourn the match while still able to stand upright.

Later, both would remember the third set as a kind of blur. After a while, it began to seem as if both were more interested in keeping the rallies going than in winning points. Fred used fewer of his cannonball serves in this set, and fewer of his crushing forehands. As his energy ebbed, he hit more and more lobs, alternating high floaters to the corners with shorter, quicker lobs nearer the middle of the court. Gloria was hitting plenty of lobs of her own; overall she was getting back pretty well anything Fred was hitting. By 3-all, the thing had evolved into a cooperative dance.

With Gloria serving for the set and match at 6-5, the thunderclaps began. Before the two could play even a dozen deuces, it was raining. At the eleventh deuce, Gloria double-faulted, for only the second time that day. Fred then returned her flat serve to his forehand with such force that she was surprised the ball had not been split in two. Six-all. The epic match had lasted over five hours.

By this time, it was raining so hard that it would have been impossible for even these intrepid souls to play any more without risking serious injury. The school buildings having been locked up tight as a drum for the summer, the two sought shelter under a tree, where they more or less fell into each others' arms, each half holding the other up. They stayed that way for ten minutes while they caught their breath. Then both declared, "It's a tie!" Emboldened by the darkness and the weather, Fred held Gloria tighter and, for the first time, planted a kiss on her lips. She responded with one of her own, and for several minutes, their two tongues dueled in an exchange fully as passionate as their tennis game had been.

As if by mutual understanding, the two broke away from each other at the same time, both saying it was time to get home for supper before their parents started to worry what had happened to them. But the epic match had wrought significant changes in Fred. Now starting to think of Gloria as perhaps something more than a tennis partner, he suggested they have their next match on Sunday morning, when he knew the store she worked in would be closed. "Then we could have a spot of lunch together," he added, putting on a note of casual sophistication.

To his surprise, she readily agreed. "I can go to mass on Saturday night," Gloria said.

"Great. So we'll meet here at 10:00 Sunday. Bring new balls—we're gonna need "em!" He emphasized this point by driving the now beat-up, waterlogged balls they'd been playing with onto the far side of the field adjacent to the parking lot.

But the next Sunday, it rained. Not just an ordinary rain, either—an almost Noah-like flood that forced not only the postponement of their tennis match, but baseball games up and down the east coast. Calling Fred at 9:00 to report the bad news, Gloria said of course she was still eager to play, and to go for lunch after the game. They rescheduled for the same time the following Sunday.

That Sunday, the 15th of July, dawned sunny but unusually cool for mid-summer. The nip in the air felt a lot more like early September. It was so chilly—only 51 according to the backyard thermometer—that Fred put on a sweater over his tennis shirt, the first time he could ever remember doing that in July. Astoundingly, he didn't feel much like eating; normally cold weather made him eat even more than usual. He had a small bowl of cereal, then lost interest and barely managed to force down a cup of coffee before getting on his bike for the 15-minute ride to the tennis courts. "Must have been that huge steak dinner we had last night," Fred said to himself in an attempt to explain his highly unusual lack of interest in breakfast. But he was far from convinced by that explanation and began to worry he might be coming down with a summer stomach flu. There had, after all, been dozens of other Saturday nights when he'd had a huge steak dinner, and yet had still been hungry enough to attack his bacon and eggs with vigor the next morning.

To his surprise—and consternation—Gloria, the ever-constant tennis keener, wasn't there when he arrived.

Normally she'd have been there for at least 10 or 15 minute before Fred was, banging a ball against the wall to practice her ground strokes. It was she who would occasionally tease him for being two or three minutes late for a game. Now the chill in his heart matched that in the air. For a few minutes, he forlornly banged one of his own balls against the wall, but soon gave this up. What the hell could have happened to her, anyway? His eyes scanned the horizon anxiously for any sign of a bike or car. Nothing. Even the birds weren't singing this frosty morning; maybe they too would rather stay in bed, he thought.

Now Fred began to feel not just worried, but angry. What could he possibly have done to deserve this? Cursing a blue streak, partly because he really did feel both angry and insulted but partly also to cover up his fears for what might have happened, Fred got on his bike at 10:30 and rode home a lot more slowly than he'd ridden to the court.

He wanted to go to the living room as soon as he got home to phone Gloria and find out what had happened. When he got there, he was in for another shock. Instead of lolling on the front terrace with the coffee pot and the Sunday *Times* as they always did during the summer months, his parents were in the living room, sitting bolt upright and talking in unusually animated fashion about an article from that august newspaper.

"Gino Cavalieri. Who'd ever have guessed?" said Fred's father, waving a section of the paper that Fred quickly recognized as the obituaries.

"Only 49, and four young kids," his mother said.

"Sure, he was carrying a few extra pounds, but who isn't, these days," his father added. "Oh, Fred," he said, noticing for the first time that his son had entered the room. "Your assistant principal just died, the *Times* says. Heart attack. He was in a hotel room in Atlantic City when it happened on Friday night. That girl you've been playing tennis with lately--"

But Fred couldn't bear to hear another word. Instead he raced upstairs to the bathroom, barely making it in time to vomit into the toilet bowl. After brushing his teeth, he went into his room and locked the door. His worried mother called up to ask him what was wrong, but his father said, "Just let him be, Lorraine. There may have been more than tennis going on there." For hours and hours, he just lay there on his bed, wishing he could cry but unable to. He felt sick to the deepest core of his being.

At 5:30, his mother said, "Your father and I are going to the McPhersons for a drink. Are you sure you'll be OK?"

"Oh, I'm OK," Fred said in a totally expressionless voice. "As OK as I'll ever be again." As soon as he heard the car pull out of the driveway, he ran down to the phone to call Gloria. Six, eight, 15 times he tried. No answer. It took him hours to get to sleep that night, and when he did sleep, he was tormented by horrific nightmares.

The next morning, he got up and vomited again. Then, after his parents had gone to work, he tried repeatedly to reach Gloria again. Still no answer. But early that afternoon, a strange, tense voice greeted him when he tried yet again.

"Mrs. Cavalieri—" Fred began cautiously.

"No, I'm not Mrs. Cavalieri. You must be Mr. Fred. I remember your voice now. I'm Thelma, the cleaning lady. She called me in this morning to clean up the house, after that terrible thing that happened to Mr. Gino. Did you hear about it?"

"Yes. My father showed me the obit in the paper. Of course, I remember your voice now, Thelma."

"She said she needed to get the house cleaned up right away, because she's going to have to sell it. Something about the insurance policy and this woman in New Jersey, and how Mr. Gino left everything to—"

Once again, Fred couldn't bear to hear another word.

"Thanks for your time. If you see Gloria, could you please ask her to call me?"

"Oh, I'm afraid I won't be seeing Gloria any more. She's gone to live in an apartment in Norwalk with her older sister. To make things easier for her mother, so she said. I won't be around much longer either. Mrs. Cavalieri said she was sorry, but she'd have to let me go after I finished cleaning the house, 'cause she just couldn't afford to keep on paying me. Broke her heart to do it—

"Goodbye, Thelma. If you do see Gloria, please ask her to call me."

"Oh, I'll certainly do that, Mr. Fred."

Fred could hardly believe what he'd just heard. It was as if someone had put a knife to his chest. A heart attack was one thing, of course; it couldn't be helped. But under these conditions, with a strange woman in a hotel room in Atlantic City? Worse still, the idea of abandoning his family for that strange woman. . .It was all Fred could do to keep from throwing up again. He spent the rest of the day in his room, mindlessly listening to the radio. At dinner, he picked at his plate for a few minutes, then pushed it away, asking to be excused.

"What on earth is wrong with you, Fred?" his mother asked. "You must be really sick. Should I phone Dr.

Moore?"

"Not much he can do for me, Mom. If you could just buy lots of ginger ale, and get used to giving me child-sized portions for a while, I'd really appreciate it. I'm afraid I really don't feel much like eating."

When he got back to his room, Fred unfortunately caught sight of his tennis racket, which was propped up in a corner of his closet. The wooden press in which he always kept it bore an autograph from Gloria. In peacock blue ink with a bold, Gothic hand, she had written, "To my favorite lob-ster of all time. Backhanded compliments to you! G.C." And now the tears did come, hesitantly, even chokingly at first as is often the case with people who don't cry very often, but soon in great, gushing torrents. Fred's entire body wracked in sobs. Several hours later, he was still crying. His mother knocked timidly at the door. "Is there anything we can do for you?" she asked.

"Yes. As a matter of fact, there is," Fred managed to get out, through his tears.

"What would that be?"

"Do you still have any of those sleeping pills Doc Moore gave you when you broke your wrist?"

"Yes, there are a few left. But I don't know if I should give you one of those. They're awfully strong—and you're awfully young."

"Unless I have something like that, I won't be able to sleep tonight. Didn't sleep worth a damn last night."

"Well, let's see what your father has to say. I know you're not one to take pills of any kind very often."

A minute or two later, she returned, carrying a small white tablet and a glass of water. "Your father and I have agreed that just this once, it's probably the best thing. You're already not eating, and if you add not sleeping to that, you might get really sick."

"Thanks, Mom. I knew you'd understand." Fred threw his arms around his mother, then downed the pill and undressed. He was still crying, though not quite as hard as before. The pill worked quickly, and in ten minutes or so, Fred had dropped off to sleep.

Fourteen hours later, Fred awakened to a cool, cloudy day. The weather matched his mood perfectly. In his heart, head, and stomach, the feeling was leaden. But he wasn't crying any more, though he came close when he caught sight of the racket again. To keep himself from more unpleasant surprises, he wrapped it up in an old jacket and shoved it into a back corner of his closet. Again he spent the day in his room listening to the radio, though he did take a few minutes to write a bit in his diary. And again that night he picked at his food and needed a sleeping pill.

Gradually, over the next couple of weeks, Fred recovered his physical strength and some of his appetite. He did, however, remain somber and withdrawn most of the time. He was glad when his father found a physically demanding job for him to do around the yard, hauling dirt and rocks in a wheelbarrow, at the then-unheard of wage of $2.00 an hour. "It will help pay for that trip to Europe you've always wanted," his father told him. The work was utterly mindless, but difficult enough physically to take his mind off the tragedy at least part of the time. By the end of August, when the job was over, he'd saved $400 and added some muscle to his already strong 190-pound frame.

If he was beginning to forget about Gloria's family, though, the New York tabloids were not. On the first of September, the *Daily News* ran a story with the headline "Cops Investigating Strange Seaside Death." On the back page continuation of the story, there was a photo of a woman who looked eerily like an older Gloria. It made his blood run cold and eventually forced him to put down the paper—not, however, before he'd learned that blackmail was one of the things the Atlantic City police were investigating.

Two days later, just as Fred was getting ready to go to New York with his mother and buy new clothes for school, he received a thick letter. The handwriting on the envelope was obviously Gloria's, though the ink was somber black rather than the peacock blue she usually favored. Inside, the letter itself was typed.

"Dear Fred," Gloria began. "I'm so, so sorry it has taken me this long to write to you. But as I'm sure you realize, it has been a very, very hard time for all of us.

"It was bad enough to lose Dad. But none of us could believe he would have done such a thing as leave that dreadful woman all his insurance. I still can't believe it— so unlike him. I was so suspicious that I talked Mom into getting a lawyer. As luck would have it, an old friend of ours who has a law office in Stamford agreed to take the case free of charge, or *pro bono* as the fancy Latin phrase he uses goes. You took Latin at prep school, didn't you? This man is like a guardian angel to us all, because he's also hired Mom as his secretary, at $100 a week. That's less than half of what Dad made, but a lot better than most secretaries, and enough to pay the basic bills. She's moved in with her older sister in Stamford for a few months, until she gets back on her feet emotionally and financially.

"As for me, I'm living with my older sister Shirley in

Norwalk now. It's a little cramped in her one-bedroom apartment, but we're making do. I've transferred to Norwalk High for next year. And I'll need to get a better job than the store job I used to have, with more hours. I'll need to work at least 20-25 hours a week if I'm to have any chance at all of going to college. So it looks as if my tennis career is on hold, at least for the time being. . .gone are my dreams of becoming the next Mo Connolly.

"Fred, I know this sounds hard, maybe even brutal, but I'm not going to send you my address or phone number, because I don't know if I could bear to see you the way I am now. . .I hope you understand. Maybe we'll meet by accident on the street in Westport. I wouldn't mind that. But it would break my heart to see you and not be able to go on playing tennis and doing the other things together that we had planned to do. You need to find a girl who won't pull you down. . ." At this point, a tear stain appeared, smearing the ink in the hitherto impeccably-presented letter.

"God bless you Fred—and goodbye. If things change, I'll be in touch, but after all of this, I don't realistically expect them to any time soon. Whatever happens, you'll always be in my heart."

Throwing the letter down on the dining-room table in

disbelief, Fred burst into another torrent of tears. He couldn't believe Gloria had said this to him. How could she be throwing such a beautiful thing as they'd had away? He was still crying when his parents returned from work several hours later. Unable to speak coherently, he showed them the letter. Then he managed to get out, "Need the sleeping pills again." This time, his mother didn't say a word, but brought a pill and a glass of water to him straight away.

The bottle was empty, and Fred was into another one, by the time he went back to school. Though he'd always hated the place in the past, this time he was actually glad to be going back. Forgotten was the earlier plan to withdraw at Christmas. Now the school was probably the best place for him, awful as it was. The harsh, sterile environment would make it easier for him to forget about Gloria. And when five tough classes and soccer or lacrosse practice weren't enough to let him do this, the bottle of bourbon he'd procured in New York would be. Lying in its place of honor beneath the dirty socks in his laundry bag, where even a bloodhound couldn't have found it, it gave him more comfort than one could imagine. Before Thanksgiving, he had replaced it twice, using day excuses to Boston as the means for doing so and having no difficulty buying the stuff openly at the famous Varsity Liquor Store in Cambridge.

He would replenish his bourbon supply ten more times during that awful year. And it seemed to help—a bit. By late October, he was no longer crying himself to sleep at night. By Christmas, he was down to one crying jag a week, and in February he was able to wean himself off the sleeping pills. Still he spent most of his days enveloped in a cloud of misery, and classmates he had previously counted as friends began to avoid him, which made him feel even worse. The psychologist and psychiatrist he consulted could do nothing for him. "It will just take time," they said. Fred respected them for being honest enough to admit they couldn't help him, but wondered if he would live long enough to overcome this crushing blow to his heart. At one point, he felt so terrible that he went to the school physician to ask for daytime tranquilizers, but on hearing some of the side effects of the medications most commonly prescribed, quickly ruled out that possibility. "Rather than take those things, I might as well jump off a bridge!" he told himself. Fortunately there were no high bridges in his immediate vicinity. But one cold, dark late-winter night, he chugged down four shots of straight bourbon in rapid succession, and prayed to the Lord, "If

You do exist, please take me out of this misery now! Stop torturing me! Give me back my Gloria, or give me instant death!" It was a good thing he no longer had the sleeping pills around. If they had been, he might well have downed the whole bottle.

Amazingly, his grades didn't suffer, at least not very much. Always a good student, Fred found a certain solace in his books and in writing, particularly his English papers. Somehow he managed to maintain a low 'B' average, with a 'D' in chemistry the only black mark on his record. He probably would have got that 'D' anyway, he told himself; as a chemist, he was a pretty good bartender.

Still concerned about his pale complexion and lack of interest in social life, his mother suggested, "Maybe this would be the time to take that trip to Europe you've been thinking about for so long," when he came home for Christmas vacation. Fred was in full agreement. Planning his destinations helped the long, cold New Hampshire nights pass more quickly. After killing three weeks in June with more mindless yard work, he left on July 4th for a whirlwind tour of most of the Continent, starting in Portugal, then working his way up through Spain, to France. Then it was on to Belgium, the Netherlands, and Denmark, before a good long stay in Germany, and shorter ones in Austria and Switzerland. From there he headed down to Italy, and then it was back to Spain and Portugal, from which he flew back to New York the day after Labor Day. To quite an extent, the trip did have the desired effect. The color was back in his cheeks, and he felt, if not cheerful, at least not horrifically miserable most of the time. And he was proud of his new knowledge of German and of wines of all sorts, from the hearty Burgundies of France to Germany's delicate, slightly sweet Rhines and Moselles.

Two things remained unchanged, though, when he returned to boarding school for his final year. He still didn't go out on dates, nor did he play any more tennis. The racket stayed in his closet, still wrapped in the old jacket. From time to time, he thought about giving it away, but the thought occurred to him that Gloria might change her mind someday, and then he'd feel terrible for having done it. And he continued to have no interest whatever in girls. On Senior Prom weekend, he went home and played bridge with his parents and a spinster friend of theirs.

With the help of even more bourbon, and now some Scotch and gin as well, Fred got through his senior year with flying colors, earning a 'B+' average and admission to four prestigious Ivy League colleges, eventually choosing

Amherst, his father's alma mater. The biggest obstacle to his graduation was getting rid of all his empty liquor bottles the morning of graduation.

Fearing that he might grow up to become, as she put it, "A wretched, solitary bachelor, living in a shabby furnished room and taking your meals alone at Bickford's Cafeteria," his mother started, during the summer after he graduated from Exeter, trying to set Fred up with dates with girls of her acquaintance. Invariably he refused, saying he'd be more than ready to go out when the time was right. And when he got to Amherst the next fall, he did start dating the girls from nearby Smith and Mount Holyoke. Most of them were pleasant enough; some were very bright; others were extremely interesting. But none came remotely close to taking his fancy the way Gloria had. Playing the field widely, he had by the end of his first year and a half at college created some dozens of future Miss Joneses. When prom time came sophomore year, he passed on it, preferring to stay in his room and work on a major English paper. Junior year he went to Boston for the weekend; senior year he spent it writing another English paper.

Gloria never wrote or called him, but at home he would see her every now and again. Always she would give a friendly wave and ask how he and his family were doing, with at least the appearance of genuine interest. And always she would say that for her part, she was doing very well. Having graduated from Norwalk High the year before, she was attending Norwalk Community College, working her way through with a job as a secretary-receptionist for a local dentist. Privately, Fred had his doubts about how well Gloria was really doing. The previously stylish, even colorful dresser now wore mainly plaid housedresses that look as if they'd come from Woolworth's bargain counter. Most of the time, she was heavily made up, which in his view didn't suit her at all. But the makeup was perhaps understandable, given that whenever she went without it, her complexion was very pale—a sign that she was still a long way from being over the tragedy.

"What do you plan to do when you finish school?" Fred asked her one time when she'd continued talking a bit longer than usual, and the old feelings of tenderness had started to well up in him.

"Oh, I really don't know. Look—I can't even think about the future. Could we not talk about it any more?"

"Why, sure—if that's the way you feel. But I'm shocked to hear you say that. A girl as sharp as you deserves to have a very bright future."

47

Tears welled up in her eyes at these words. She was unable to speak. Fred took her in his arms and gave her a close hug. She did not resist, but broke away after a minute or two. "Maybe we *should* talk about this some more," she said. "But now I've got to get back to work. See you sooner rather than later, I hope."

As it turned out, though, the two didn't see each other for several months, and when they did again run into each other on the street, she showed no interest at all in resuming the subject. Fred wasn't happy to let it drop, but he had to respect her space, and resolved not to bring it up again until she did. The result was that in their increasingly infrequent meetings, they would do little more than exchange pleasantries, delicately skating around any deeper issues.

Midway through Fred's college years, his parents rented an apartment in New York, where his mother had started graduate work in political science. This meant that he was no longer spending much time in Westport, since the family would go out there only for weekends and Christmas and summer vacations. Now he was only seeing Gloria about once a year. Always she would wave at him, gaily, and look as if she would like to talk but couldn't spare the time just then. So they didn't talk. Although he'd been have glad enough to pursue something with her, he found her general bearing more than a little forbidding in her general bearing toward him, and therefore refrained from trying to do more.

When he was 25, his parents sold the Westport house. Now he had little reason ever to go to his old home town. In addition, he'd married one of his fellow Cornell graduate students, and they'd had a daughter. This meant that time and money for travel were both at a premium. Both became even scarcer when Fred and his wife divorced just three years into the marriage.

During a 22-year period—from age 27 to age 49—Fred set foot in Westport exactly three times, one of them being for his father's funeral. His remarriage at 37 left him still less time for solitary travel, and his appetite for nostalgia was sufficiently satisfied if he stopped for lunch at one of his old haunts every seven or eight years while on the way to or from northern New England. He thought about Gloria a lot during these visits, it must be admitted, especially after being divorced a second time at age 45, but still made no attempt to contact her. His teaching job at Williams kept him busy; he had plenty of interests; and there *were* women in his life—let's let it go at that for now.

Meanwhile, as he'd heard through a friend, Gloria had at 31 married an older man named Bob Brown who owned a hat factory in Waterbury and was worth several million. A nice guy, so the report went, but completely uninterested in the arts or most other finer things in life and in fact stupefyingly dull. A Republican who played golf three times a week and wouldn't think of having dinner without a martini first. Shades of Scarlett O'Hara and Frank Kennedy, Fred wondered? In any event, free of the need to work for a living, Gloria had evidently become completely immersed in the suburban housewife routine, ferrying kids to and from school, music lessons, soccer games, and keeping a nice home, one her husband could be proud of when he brought business associates around for drinks or dinner. At first, Fred wondered how long Gloria would last with this kind of life, thinking that such a vital woman would surely go mad out of sheer boredom. But he soon put those reflections away. . .for whatever reasons, this was the life she had decided to live, and he would have to respect that.

On his first and second 'midlife' visits, Fred didn't see Gloria at all. But on the last one, he did see her, walking on the other side of the town's main street. What he saw troubled his soul. There, walking ever so slowly on the nearly-empty sidewalk, was a woman in her late 40's who looked at least 60. He knew from her face that it had to be her, but couldn't believe she could possibly look that old and worn-out. She wore a heavy mink stole that seemed to drag her down every step of the way. In each of her hands she carried a huge shopping bag filled with parcels. The way she was carrying them, they looked more like bricks than the Christmas presents they almost certainly were. She looked for all the world like a character out of *Les Parapluies de Cherbourg*—except that the setting was suburban New York, not France. The one telltale sign of life (in addition to her long, still-black hair) was the sway in her hips. (Thank God for that token of continuing life and vitality, which meant there was still *some* hope for her). At this point, he parked his car and crossed the street to talk to her.

"Hi, Gloria. I've been thinking a lot about you lately. How have things been going with you?"

She looked up at her old tennis partner with an expression of such utter, abject misery that it tore his heart to see it. "Oh, you don't want to know. You really don't want to know."

"Would it help if I lent you a shoulder to cry on? For just an hour or so, while we have a cup or two of coffee and do some catching-up? I've been divorced twice and was rejected for tenure three times before finally getting it, so I think I know something about pain myself."

"I—well no, I just couldn't. Can't inflict myself on anybody when I'm like this. It's all just too awful."

"Are you sure?" Fred asked with real concern. "Holding stuff like that in isn't good for you, you know."

Instead of replying, Gloria burst into tears—the long, slow, anguished kind that come from a place very deep in one's being. To which Fred's response was to throw his arms around her, after somehow managing to free her of the parcels, and hold her tight against him. For five, ten, fifteen minutes and more he held her there, despite being bareheaded and gloveless on the chilly January afternoon.

Did all this make Gloria feel any better? Without a retrospective crystal ball, such a question is impossible to answer. I do know that she made no attempt to free herself from his arms, and I also know that by the end of twenty minutes, the initial torrent of tears had been reduced to an intermittent trickle. Finally, I know that at the end it was Fred who broke free of the embrace—not Gloria, who truth to tell might well have stayed there all afternoon had he not suddenly broken away.

"Oh, my God. I completely forgot. I'm supposed to be giving a talk at a meeting in Williamstown in five hours—and I haven't even prepared it yet. Damn it! I wish we could go have dinner somewhere. Now, Gloria, we really must keep in touch this time, no matter what." With that he kissed her fiercely on the lips, then gave her a final hug and thrust two business cards into the pocket of her mink, one bearing his work address and the other his home address. "Now you'll have no excuses for not contacting me," he said, feigning gaiety as if he had just run into a casual acquaintance. "Toodle-ooh."

Throughout the long, somewhat hazardous drive back to Williamstown, made even more hazardous by his having to drive 15 miles above the speed limit most of the way to make it back on time, he fantasized about what would happen if he found a message from her on his answering machine. Alas! it wasn't about to happen. She never called or wrote him, let alone suggested a visit. After three years or so, he resigned himself to the thought that he would probably never see her again.

But he did in fact run across her again, though it happened by pure chance. In his mid 50's, Fred had left teaching to become a full-time novelist. On the strength of decent (though not overwhelming) sales for his first novel, he decided to get an agent to market his second, and accordingly contacted Dalton's, a New York literary agency that a friend of his had used with some success. A month later, the head of the agency telephoned him personally.

"Your works clearly have literary merit," old Mr. Dalton had said. "I think they have commercial possibilities, too, though those possibilities are not quite so immediately apparent as in the case of certain other, how shall I put it, flashier writers."

"Not flashy is good," Fred said. "I can't compete with Tom Clancy or Anne Rice—and I don't even propose to try!"

"Quite so. But you do need to get in with a firm with some marketing savvy; that's why I think you made a good decision contacting us. And I've decided to assign you to the best of our newer agents, Gloria Brown (I can't say younger, she only started about five years ago as a career switch). More than anyone else we have, she knows how to take a book with real merit and make it appear, how shall I say, sexy to potential publishers. I fully expect to see some Pulitzers emerge from her work with us.

"Just one thing I'd better warn you about, right off the bat. Gloria has had a tough life, and initially she can come across as very reserved—even not interested in the person she's talking to. By times, she can also be a bit prickly. New England background, you know. But as you work with her more, you'll learn first-hand just how fine a literary mind she has, and how dedicated an agent she is.

"If all this is acceptable to you, then, I'll put your contract in the mail this afternoon. Nothing very unusual about it—we take the standard 10% but cover most of the reasonable expenses and even a few of the unreasonable ones. So long as you don't ask us for 5000 pages of photocopying in color and on short notice, we can probably live with your requests.

"I guess the only question left is when can you come in to see us and, above all, meet Gloria," Dalton concluded. He asked if Fred would be free the following Thursday, at 2:00. He would. In preparation for this meeting, Fred booked his return train ticket and sent his best sportcoat and grey flannels to the cleaner.

Fred made sure to arrive 20 minutes early, so he would have time to "case out the joint" and see if he felt comfortable in his new agents' offices. To a surprising degree, he did. The offices were old and spacious. The large waiting room to which he was ushered by a friendly and far from unhip receptionist reminded him of a good men's club or university faculty club. The shelves were lined with books (most though not all by authors whom Dalton's had worked with over the years), and three coffee tables were tastefully covered by magazines of a suitably literary nature. Clearly then, at the macro level, the place worked. All that was left was to meet this Gloria Brown woman and see how he clicked with her.

He recognized her instantly when she walked in the door, wearing a tweed skirt and slightly baggy wool sweater—the sort of outfit that the female teachers of their day would have worn in class. Though the outfit camouflaged her still-excellent figure, it couldn't hide the sway in the hips, which went on at a merrier rate than ever, much to Fred's secret delight.

"Well, I'll be damned," he said, shaking his head in amazement at the transformation his old friend had undergone. "Isn't this a pleasant surprise?"

Damn it, had she noticed the way he was looking at her? She had this quizzical, slightly stern look in her eyes that he seemed to remember from almost as far back as he'd known her. "No funny business," she said, as soon as Fred had seated himself in an overstuffed leather armchair facing her spacious desk.

"I wouldn't be capable of it any more, at my advanced age."

"Somehow I'm not so sure about that," she laughed. "Just giving you a heads-up."

"Why—are you still married or something like that. No one I know is still married. And is your last name really Brown? Somehow that doesn't seem to suit you. You're a Cavalieri, full of Latin vim and vigor, not some dull plain vanilla WASP like me."

"Thanks for the compliment," Gloria said, with a bit of the old flash in her eye. "You've actually got plenty of spice mixed in with that vanilla yourself. And, no, I'm definitely not married any more. Finally won my freedom nine years ago, after two decades of living hell. But I got enough money out of him to launch out on my own. Bought a house in Westport and set up my one-horse agent studio. Stuck with it for a couple of years, until I realized there were a lot of problems involved with running my own business. So I got Dalton's to take me on, on the strength of the work I'd been doing. Now I have many of the benefits of being on my own, and very few of the drawbacks. A regular salary and benefits are nice things to have. As for the name, that's just a matter of convenience—and plain, simple laziness. Having taken my husband's name in the first place, which admittedly may have been a big mistake, I simply couldn't see taking the time and trouble to change everything back. Not to mention that 'Brown' is a much easier name for clients to printers to put on business cards, etc."

an see your point about the name. But just

.y, why all this concern about funny business?

ʋʋ ᵘ˸   ɩg signs of engaging in it, or something?"

" Not at all. It's just that, given our past history—oh, I can't say any more right now." For just a moment, raw anguish burst through Gloria's carefully composed (and now heavily made-up) face. Fred's heart began to melt anew, as her expression brought back to him they way she'd looked the last time they had met, in Westport. But Fred took pains not to take advantage, breaking up the potentially awkward moment with some casual humor.

" I understand. The business of America is business. And remember: we are not in business for our health. It is the dollars we are after."

"Spoken like a true disciple of Andrew Carnegie. At least he did set up some pretty decent libraries across the country with all his ill-gotten gains. Now, the good news is that I've become rather adept at my work, after a slow start. So if it's the dollars you are indeed after, stick with me and Dalton's, and you should have a fair pile of them. Enough at least for a farm in the Poconos, if not that villa in the south of France you used to joke about retiring to."

"Sounds good to me. My pension is only about $1600

a month, and I sure don't want to have to go back to teaching freshman comp to pay for my daughter's orthodontist bills. Just one more question, Gloria. Do you still play tennis?"

Damn it all, there was that heart-rending gaze of utter misery again, just when Fred thought they'd got past all of that. Fortunately, Gloria recovered more quickly this time. "Haven't given it up, but I have put it on hold for a while. For now I haven't got the time, though I'd really like to get back to the game again. Bob—that's my ex--was always playing—and always hanging out at the club. Usually came home around midnight pissed as a newt. Believe me, the tennis balls weren't all he was making a play for—oh, Jesus, there I go again!"

"Later, over a drink," Fred said in a tone he *hoped* was soothing.

"After you sell us your next book," Gloria replied, putting on her best attempt at a stern look. "We'll do it by way of cementing the deal."

Eight months later, they still hadn't gone for that drink. But no one could deny that Fred and Gloria were an effective team. More than a mere agent, she was an expert literary advisor who knew just which commercially successful bells and whistles to suggest he insert into his novels—and when to lay off on those kinds of suggestions. Initially he'd resisted, and there'd been two or three quietly fierce battles around the boardroom table in Dalton's, Fred arguing for artistic integrity and Gloria arguing, equally passionately, for things that would appeal to a larger audience. An alarming increase in his household and child support expenses had on several occasions led him to concede "just for this one book." If he was really unhappy with the results, he, Gloria, and old Mr. Dalton agreed, they would do the third novel *his* way, with no gimmicks or compromises of any kind.

By this time, Fred was beginning to suspect that artistic integrity, at least as he had known it, might just be on the way to becoming a thing of the past. Having gone along with her suggestions of shorter chapters, a lighter tone and a scene, involving a rock video, that would definitely appeal to a younger audience than he had hitherto written for, he had seen his novel, *Getting It On,* immediately picked up by Random House. Both the Book of the Month Club and Oprah selected it. Before the year was out, sales had reached six digits. In another six months, royalties were such that Fred knew that, if he only took care to handle his money just a little bit carefully, he would never, ever even have to think about teaching freshman composition again.

His third novel, *Warding Them Off,* attracted considerable interest in Hollywood, and Gloria was able to negotiate a fat movie-rights contract in addition to another excellent deal with Random House. Though the movie, when it was eventually made, was only a moderate commercial success, it somehow managed to pique readers' interest in the novel, to the extent that sales this time were in the seven-digit range by the end of two years. Not only was Fred able to pay off his daughter's orthodontist bill; he bought his farm (in the Berkshires rather than the Poconos) along with a shiny new silver Mercedes sedan, and took on a stockbroker. Though he couldn't yet quite afford to buy the much-talked-about villa in the south of France, he did arrange for an annual six-week time share on one, which would do until his next novel came out. Now, unless he did something downright stupid with his money, he would never need to earn another cent. The interest on what he had saved up would allow for an extremely comfortable if not extravagant lifestyle. Best of all, he was now free to write whatever he wanted, however he wanted.

To his surprise, as he contemplated a shift back toward the kind of novels he'd dreamed of writing when he was a struggling young English professor, he found that Gloria agreed with him completely. "You've got all the money anyone could reasonably need in this world. Why not write what you want? The time will never be better." She was now senior partner, old Mr. Dalton having retired the previous year. Somehow, this made Fred listen to her advice just a bit more intently. But just to show she hadn't taken her eye completely off the "main chance," she renegotiated his standard contract to insert an "escalator clause," whereby the agent's cut would be reduced slightly for each 100,000 copies sold after an initial 500,000. "So you're telling me to do what I want, but if I write you a blockbuster you'll make it worth my while," Fred laughed.

"Something like that," agreed Gloria, with a little laugh of her own. Fred was glad to see the sparkle back in her eyes, nearly as strong as it had been when she was his after-school tennis partner. He was on the verge of asking her if she was free for tennis or at least a drink that weekend when the phone rang, and Gloria's expression told him it was a call she needed to take. Remembering how much she had enjoyed male companionship even at age 14, he found himself hoping fervently that it wasn't an unattached man over 45 on the other end of the line. He was slightly though not totally reassured when she put down the phone just as he was putting on his coat and gave him a spontaneous hug, for the first time ever in their new partnership. Could this be the sign he'd been waiting for for so long? Still he refrained from asking her out, fearful of rejection and of spoiling what appeared to be, ever so slowly, becoming a good thing.

"Just my daughter," Gloria said, to Fred's great relief, as he was walking out the door. "She's in town and wants to do dinner tonight."

Determined to prove to his agent that he could still write a novel that would be an artistic as well as commercial success, Fred retreated to his farm just as the leaves were starting to turn and started putting in long hours on his fourth novel, *Head for the Hills*. The book was about a middle-aged couple from New York who'd discovered their love for each other at a summer tennis camp in Western Massachusetts. Whether it was the thrice-weekly dreams he was having about Gloria, or his desire to finish the novel in time to spend most of the winter at that villa in the south of France, Fred wrote at a furious pace, almost in fact rivaling that of D.H. Lawrence, who is said to have written the 400-plus page epic *Kangaroo* in just over six weeks. (In fairness, Fred's IBM computer did provide him with a certain technological edge over Lawrence's manual typewriter). He finished the 380-page book two days after Thanksgiving.

A week later, he was meeting with Gloria to hear her suggestions for revision. They were well-thought-out as always, but this time Fred was impressed mainly by how few of them there were, compared to his two previous novels. He was also impressed by what appeared to be a new look in her eye, one not just of professional respect but of admiration, perhaps even awe. By mid-December, he'd finished the minor revisions she'd requested. Gloria wasted no time in shipping the MS out to Random House, who gave them an even better deal on the film rights than they had before. The deal was signed, sealed and delivered just after New Year's, which would give Fred lots of time to relax in his rented villa, and gird his loins for the rigors of the reading tour that awaited him come spring and summer.

"Would you consider taking me with you?" Gloria asked, teasingly, as they finally enjoyed the long-awaited drink at the Algonquin the night before his flight to Paris. Both were dressed extremely elegantly, in a casual way, she in tight black pants and a pink cashmere sweater, he in corduroy jeans, a black turtleneck and a new houndstooth check sport jacket he'd bought specifically for the reading series.

"Oh, I'd definitely consider it," he said. "But are you ready for six weeks of heavy leisure, broken only by the odd swim and occasional tennis game?"

Though he'd spoken casually, his words were clearly having an impact on her; he could in fact see the struggle in her face. Gloria would make the world's worst bank robber, he thought; her face would never let her get away with anything. Right now, she was close to bursting into tears. And this caused some conflict in Fred. Though with all his heart he wanted to reach out to her, comfort her, let her know how much she meant to him, something else told him now was the time to play hard to get. The ball, after all, was definitely in her court. When, after a very long pause, she still hadn't replied, Fred said lightly, "Of course, if you're too busy to go right now, I understand perfectly. . .but the offer will still be open."

"Maybe I shouldn't quite yet," she said, in a voice which startled him with its huskiness. "The new Maldonado thriller will be coming in next week, and I have to sell that. Then, of course, there's your reading tour to plan. But if there's an emergency, I'll certainly call you. Have no fear of that."

"As you wish," he said. They touched glasses and exchanged quick kisses in the French style, on both cheeks but not on the lips.

"See you soon!" Gloria said as they left the hotel.

Fred's only reply was to wink flirtatiously. He himself was on the brink of tears, and he didn't sleep at all well, nearly missing his early morning flight.

Five weeks later, at the villa, he was shocked to get a late-evening call from Gloria. "It *is* an emergency," she said, "so I'm calling in my chips."

"Why, what's wrong?"

"Random House is bringing out two more big books than usual this spring, so they need to get yours out a month ahead of schedule. With the new "just-in-time" printing technology, they can now do this quite easily. They've already printed 50,000, and another 50,000 are ready to go literally at a day's notice. This means your reading tour has to be moved up, or critical sales momentum will be lost."

"So?"

"So this means you're opening in Boston a week from Tuesday. From there it's on to Providence, New Haven, Stamford, and New York. Then you'll go down the coast—you can keep on using Amtrak if you want, they might even want you to read in the dining car--then out to New Orleans, back north to Chicago and through the Midwest, and out to the Pacific Coast by way of Denver. We're just hitting the high spots for now. We can do the smaller places, like northern New England, in the late spring or early summer."

"And the South?" he asked with some concern.

"Oh, not to worry. Now that you're an Established Name, we have the luxury of pretty much passing on the Sahara of the Bozart. Richmond, Atlanta, Miami, and New Orleans are your only southern stops for the whole tour."

"I can't tell you how much it breaks my heart that I won't be reading in Tupelo, Mississippi, Anniston, Alabama, or Little Rock, Arkansas," he laughed. "Not to mention Houston, Fort Worth-Dallas, and Oklahoma City."

"Somehow, I suspect you'll survive those admittedly serious omissions," Gloria said, with a twinkle in her voice that made him long to be with her. "And so, in fact, will we."

"All the same, it makes me tired just hearing about this reading tour," Fred said much more seriously. "I'm not all that well-rested, you know. For some reason, I haven't been sleeping that well."

"Me neither. Isn't that funny? I wonder why. Too much coffee, maybe?"

"Not any more. I limit myself strictly to three cups a day, and I've even started putting milk in it the way the French do."

"I've been more careful than usual about my coffee as well. Strange. We'll have to talk about it when we get back. Oh, and by the way—you won't have to change your reservation. I had my assistant do that earlier today. You'll be taking the 4 p.m. flight out of De Gaulle tomorrow."

This was all a bit too much for Fred to handle, especially on short notice. "How in the world—"

"Oh, I phoned the airline—you'd told me which one you were flying out on—and told them we'd just heard your sister was gravely ill in New York. Tomorrow afternoon's flight was the first one we could get you in on. You'll have to catch the morning train out of Marseille— 8:00 I think it is. We've booked that for you as well."

"This is *highly* irregular. They didn't ask for medical evidence or anything?"

"Medical evidence? Are you kidding? What I ask for, I usually get."

"I appreciate that. Well—OK. I, er, hope this isn't going to set a precedent. I really could have used the extra week of rest. This last year has been a tough one."

"For me, too," Gloria said sympathetically. "For me, too. But somehow I have the feeling *this* year will be a better one for both of us. And now, dear boy, you had better go and get some rest. Someone from Dalton's will be meeting you at the airport. There are things I need to discuss with you before the tour, and I thought we might as well get that out of the way day after tomorrow, to allow you at least a few days at the farm to prepare. So they'll meet you and take you to a downtown hotel, then on Friday we can meet for a late breakfast in the dining room and take it from there"

"Whew!" said Fred, exhausted at the thought of the weeks ahead of him. "Well, goodnight." As he headed to the dining room sideboard for a pre-bedtime brandy, he noticed that he'd felt genuine sadness at hanging up the phone. Had Gloria felt that same sadness, he wondered? And would someone from the airline be meeting him at the gate as well, just to keep him honest? Oh well. If that happened, he guessed it would be easy enough just to tell him his sister had died during the night. By comparison with what Gloria had already pulled off, that little white lie would be a piece of cake.

Much to his surprise, it was Gloria herself who met him at the airport, looking positively ravishing in tight jeans, knee-length leather boots and a scarlet turtleneck that left little to the imagination, under a stylish black leather jacket. "How do you manage to look so good at 61?" Fred asked.

"Just luck—and genes," she laughed. "My mother's, not my father's. I haven't been exercising much at all since I stopped playing tennis." They embraced, but she quickly disengaged herself. "No funny business tonight," she said. "I'm driving you to the hotel. It's the Algonquin—hope you won't mind--and our business meeting will start there at 10:00 tomorrow morning, in the dining room. Bring your best appetite! What we can't take care of there, we'll discuss back at the office. Hopefully we can get it all out of the way by 3:00, because my son is flying in from Colorado tomorrow for the weekend."

Gloria's black Mercedes sports car barely had room for the two of them, so Fred was forced to send his luggage over to the hotel by taxi. To his surprise—he had always thought of her as sensible and cautious—she drove the Mercedes like a race-car driver. His heart was pumping hard by the time they arrived at the Algonquin, and not *just* because of his feelings for her. "When do you plan to do the Daytona Salt Flats?" he asked, only partially in jest.

"Maybe in my next incarnation," she laughed. "But the West Side Highway is a pretty fair substitute—wouldn't you agree?"

How he wished he could share his lovely little room at the Algonquin with his beautiful, sexy agent. But she wouldn't hear of it, though she did, with a show of reluctance, agree to a quick drink in the bar. Then, his luggage having in the meantime arrived, she abandoned him to the bellhop in the lobby, giving him the sort of quick, dry peck on the cheek a suburban matron might give her husband at the train station. "Don't forget to be there at 10:00 sharp!" she said. His nerves more than a little on edge after the last two weeks of emotional upheaval, Fred couldn't stop his racing mind and eventually resorted to a sleeping pill, awaking just in time to shower, shave and dress, and grab a quick coffee before the meeting.

The meeting went by in a blur. Arriving at the dining room at 9:58, Fred found Gloria already there, dressed in a heavy grey tweed suit and sturdy black Oxfords that went well with it, looking like a senior social work supervisor from the Harry Truman years. Enough papers to fill a large briefcase were spread out on the table all around her, though there was no briefcase in sight. When her lox, bagel, and cream cheese arrived, she attacked them vigorously. Fred, on the other hand, merely toyed with his cheese omelette. Before long he'd pushed his plate away altogether, contenting himself with occasional sips of coffee.

Seemingly oblivious to Fred's discomfiture, Gloria went on quoting sales and royalty projections, train schedules, and hotel locations at a great rate. She certainly had it all in hand, he thought—and a good thing, too. His brain was literally fried with this welter of practical detail. Throughout the 90-minute meeting, he said next to nothing, only nodding occasionally to show that he'd heard or saying, "Yes," or, at most, "I see."

Then, as quickly as it had begun, the meeting was over. "Is there anything else you think we need to discuss?" Gloria asked.

"Not a thing. All I need now is some sleep. I'll call you from the farm the night before I leave for the tour." Another chaste, wifely peck on the cheek and she was gone, promising to see him again when the tour reached New York. As he boarded his farm-bound train, he found himself impatiently awaiting that next meeting, and quite unable to focus on the details of the forthcoming reading tour.

All the same, his first two readings, at Harvard and the Boston Public Library, gave Fred the assurance that people really liked his book. Though he'd always been a fine public reader, he exceeded himself on these two occasions. The Providence YMCA event was a bit of a letdown, but his spirits were renewed by the warm reception he received both at Yale and in the public library at Stamford, the town in which he'd been born so many years ago. After selling nearly a hundred books at the Stamford reading, Fred treated himself to a seafood dinner at a nearby restaurant and triumphally boarded a train for Grand Central and New York, where he would, he trust, meet Gloria once again.

Despite all his earlier triumphs, though, Fred found himself in a foul mood as he left his room at the Chuzzlewit Hotel on New York's Lower East Side to go out for a spot of lunch before his Saturday reading. First off, why had she booked him into this seedy, unknown little joint rather than his beloved Algonquin? With sales going through the roof (by her own admission), Dalton's certainly had the money to do better. Beyond that, she knew that Fred disliked weekend readings on principle, so why would she have booked him for not just one, but two? First, there would be the reading in the Chuzzlewit's library, at 1:30 on Saturday. Then, on Sunday afternoon, he had been booked in for a reading at a bookstore on Staten Island in a town called Tottenville he had once visited, on some misguided whim. It was a place at the very end of the subway line, where half-mad dogs roamed the streets, and the few people on those largely deserted streets looked at him more than a little suspiciously. A sort of Appalachia within Metro New York. Why on earth had she booked him into such a hellhole? But above all, when was he going to see her again. At the thought of her, his heart began racing, to the point where he was considering taking one of his sleeping pills as a daytime tranquilizer. But realizing that the pill would make it hard for him to read well, he took a couple dozen deep breaths, which allowed him to regain enough composure to continue with his day.

Quickly dispatching a bowl of clam chowder at a nearby Chock Full O'Nuts—he had never been one to expend much time or energy on lunch—Fred paid, then strode smartly out the door to head over to 5th Avenue for the brisk half-hour walk he always took before a reading, to clear his head and to make his final decision on which selections to include. Turning left to head downtown, he was pleased to see a small but energetic anti-Iraq war demonstration outside the New York Public Library on 42nd St. It did his heart good to see that at least some of today's young people still had the idealism and feistiness that he and his friends had had back in the Vietnam era. Fred waved cheerfully at the demonstrators before heading down to 34th St., which was as far as he dared go given his time constraints.

His earlier annoyance quickly vanished upon his return to the Chuzzlewit. Indeed, he soon realized there had been some method to Gloria's madness after all. It turned out that the hotel, which he'd never heard of before, was a haven for all sorts of local artistic activity, particularly literary activity, much of which was conducted in a library deep in the bowels of the building's basement. Its high ceilings, heavy, dark furniture, and book-lined shelves made him feel right at home. So many enthusiastic listeners filled the library that more chairs had to be brought in to accommodate everyone. After a few more deep breaths, Fred launched into his reading and was quickly lost in his own work, surprising even himself with his enthusiastic performance. And could that have been Gloria there in the back, winking at him flirtatiously as he read?

It turned out that everyone liked his book so much that he was forced to give two encores before the crowd finally dispersed. After this triumphal reading, which had been followed by 40 sales, Fred had expected a modest peck on the cheek or sisterly hug from his agent and friend, who'd waited till everyone else was gone to congratulate him. Instead, to his great surprise and secret delight, he found himself being gently but firmly grabbed by a belt loop and pulled over to a side wall in a dark corridor outside the reading room. There Gloria used her knee to separate his blue-jeaned legs, ramming him into the wall with a strength he hadn't known she still possessed, and kissing him more passionately than he'd ever been kissed before. Keeping her hand on his belt loop, she led him out of the auditorium where he'd just done his reading, through the hotel's labyrinth of passageways, and into the lobby.

Never relaxing her grip, Gloria guided him into the service elevator, which had appeared quickly and mysteriously.

"What the he—" demanded Fred.

"Sh!" said Gloria, gripping him even harder down below and using her other arm to pull him close for a fierce embrace. To which he responded in kind, pressing her breasts against his chest and covering her face with kisses.

"Aren't you glad this hotel has an extra slow service elevator?" Gloria laughed.

Now it was his turn to silence her—by kissing her some more.

There being little demand for the services of the service elevator late on a Saturday afternoon, the two were able to ride the elevator up and down half a dozen times or more, wrapped around each other, until on the seventh or eighth trip a little bell went off, just as they were nearing Fred's room on the 18th floor.

"Hate to break off this abruptly, but you know how it is," Fred said. He couldn't help noticing, while looking into the mirror across from the elevator, that both their eyes were glistening with tears of joy, both had bright red cheeks, and that Gloria's thick black hair seemed to be struggling to break free of its clasp. As well, both their voices were husky and just the slightest bit hoarse.

"I understand.

"Tell you what. I just need a little time to get my head straight. Come back in an hour and we'll have a drink. I'm in 1812.

"Isn't that convenient? I'm just down the hall in 1818.

"Toodle-ooh," he said, grabbing her for a final brief, though fierce embrace.

Little did Gloria know that getting his head together was probably the least of Fred's worries. For once in his life, it was right where he wanted it to be. Getting everything done he needed to get done in the allotted hour was going to be the challenge.

After hanging up his sportcoat and tie, he quickly showered and shaved, making sure to do a thorough job on the chin and above his upper lip. Then he changed to clean jeans, boots and a denim work shirt. Forty-five minutes to go. Pausing briefly at the front desk, he asked the desk clerk to get an ice bucket and some linen napkins sent up to his room. From there, it was on to the jeweler's, two blocks away at 49th St. He made it just minutes before the store's 5:00 closing. Apologizing for his late arrival, he asked to see the engagement rings. There were several hundred on display, but most were much too fancy and frilly for his taste. One section, though, contained nothing but plain gold bands. It was this section to which he now gave his undivided attention, quickly settling on a slim band at once strong and delicate—like Gloria herself, he thought.

"Do you know what size she takes?" asked the jeweler.

"I'm afraid not," laughed Fred. "But I'm guessing something mid-range."

"If you could tell me how tall she is, how much she weighs, and what her body build is, it might help."

Fred gave the jeweler all that information, based on his best scientific guesstimates.

"Sounds like mid-range is indeed your best bet," the latter said. "But you can always bring it back and exchange it if it doesn't fit. We've got lots more of these in stock."

"That's good to know," Fred replied.

The sale complete, he put the ring, encased in a lovely little black box, into a front pocket and raced off in search of a liquor store. It was now 5:10. He needed to be back in his room in 20 minutes. Evidently New Yorkers were not drinking so much as they had in the past, because it took him a while to find a liquor store. He had to go four blocks down, to 45th, and one block over, to 1st Avenue, to find one.

Clearly the occasion called for champagne. Nothing less would do. After only brief thought on the matter, he asked for, and was given, a bottle of Mumm's Extra Dry.

No sooner had his purchase been paid for and bagged then Fred started racing back toward the hotel. It was now 5:20, and the hotel was seven and a half blocks away. The last thing he wanted, at this point, was to be late for Gloria.

Alternating between walking and running, he pushed himself so hard that by the time he reached the hotel lobby at 5:28, the denim shirt was as sweaty as the one he'd taken off just an hour earlier. He really should change it, he thought, as he waited anxiously for the elevator. His anxiety only increased as the elevator slowly wended its way up to the 18th floor, letting off a succession of kids, grandparents, comfortable and not so comfortable middle-aged couples, and the odd young couple.

By the time he was finally deposited on the 18th floor, it was 5:31. No sooner had he left the elevator and turned right than he literally ran into Gloria, dressed to kill in a black skirt and rainbow-colored peasant blouse, with black flats. She did her best to keep a stern look on her face, but seeing his obvious discomfiture, was barely restraining herself from laughing.

"Couldn't find a liquor store in this place for love or money. Had to go eight blocks to find one," he said.

"Sh!" Gloria said for the second time that day. This time, her tone was tender beyond words. "Lay down your burdens at my feet," she whispered. Then she grabbed him and gave him a long, lingering, and exceptionally passionate kiss.

He had been planning to wait to propose to her until they got into the hotel room and were nicely settled with their champagne. But finding himself overwhelmed by her passion, and awestruck by her beauty, he realized he couldn't wait even that long. After following her deep, passionate kiss with an even deeper and more passionate one of his own, he knelt at her feet and asked her to marry him.

Without a second's hesitation, she said "Yes," then pulled him up to standing position, again grabbing him by the belt loop, and led him to the door of his room, which, given all the distractions, he did very well to get open.

Much to his surprise and delight, Fred felt no awkwardness whatever around Gloria once she'd agreed to marry him, even though he had done no more than kiss her up till now. It was as if he'd been making love to her every week for 20 years, rather than attempting it for the first time.

No sooner had Gloria entered the bedroom than Fred undid her long black skirt, in a single deft gesture that was nothing short of masterful. For her part, Gloria celebrated her liberation from the garment with a slow, undulating dance, of the sort that deserves tambourines for accompaniment and glowing incense sticks as a backdrop.

Fred responded as men have responded to such dances from time immemorial, by taking the dancer into his arms and hugging and kissing her and then continuing with a little under-the-waist undulation of his own.

Next to go (after his jeans) was Gloria's bright, rainbow-colored silk blouse. This time, Fred was slow, almost tender in the way he unbuttoned the garment. It was she who showed the slightest sign of impatience, by flinging the blouse to the floor as soon as he'd reached the bottom button. Stripped to her bra and panties, Gloria added to the air of abandon by unclipping her long black hair, letting the shoulder-length tresses cascade all over her face—and his. Just seeing her like this and feeling her hair flying in his face made Fred want to pick her up, throw her on the bed and make passionate love to her, but something in him told him discretion would be the better part of valor just then. After a suitable pause for another gypsy-like dance, she undid his blue denim work shirt a lot more rapidly and roughly than he had undone her blouse.

Decisions, decisions. Would her bra or panties be next? It was she who made the decision for him, by shaking her breasts in such a way that he knew that whatever was holding them in would have to go. Stealing a leaf from her book, Fred was more forceful in his removal of the bra, without in any way sacrificing his earlier grace. Now they were dancing together, Fred using the bra as a sort of prop as well as a foil for the slow, intense wiggling of Gloria's breasts. Though fuller than they had been in her youth, they were still not large, but she made every bit of them count as she gyrated.

In perfect synchronicity, each continued to move while reaching for, then slowly stripping the underpants off the other. Gradually the slow dance evolved into an erotic massage, as they moved nipple to chest, then thigh to thigh, butt to butt, and finally in a full-body embrace that took the breath away from both.

Overcome by a passion that had taken more than four decades to build up, Fred tenderly, indeed almost tentatively inserted his penis into Gloria's vagina. She responded with a deft series of pelvic thrusts that by themselves were almost enough to push him past the brink. Then he kissed her as he had never kissed her or any other woman before, thrusting deep into her throat with his tongue as they continued to sway to the timeless, silent music. . .

They had their first orgasm that way, standing up, and they had it together. Then they stood quite still for a while, savoring the moment before gently beginning to run their hands through each other's hair. Then Gloria deftly curled her hips around Fred's, motioning toward the bed.

"We're paying $150 a night for this—might as well use it," she said.

Soon she was straddling him, thrusting those supple hips vigorously as she slowly moved her body up and down his in a sort of swimming motion. Faced by this irresistible force of nature, Fred could do no more than submit. Sixty-year-olds aren't supposed to be able to achieve a second orgasm less than half an hour after the first. . .so at least said all his sex books. But Fred must have forgotten to read that part of the books. Soon after Gloria started working on him, he was lying in delicious agony at the brink. (She had stopped, momentarily, to draw out the experience). A minute or so later, after a finale that would have made the "William Tell Overture" sound tame, he was screaming out his passion for her, and she hers for him, her now-damp hair covering his face and making him think of her body as a kind of mossy treehouse to which he had somehow managed to escape. For half an hour or more, they lay still, he inside her, tears of joy and cosmic relief streaming down their faces.

He didn't believe he could possibly have anything left in him, but when she started in on her gypsy dance yet again, what could he do but rise to attention? Now it was him on top of her, the missionary of mature love, again starting slow but building to a frenzied climax, using every trick in his book and muscle in his body to please his lady love. And again they came together.

This time, though, there were no shrieks, no cries of animal passion. The climax came so quickly, like a surprise sunset after rain on an August day, that both were completely overwhelmed. With him still inside her, they blacked out almost immediately.

"We need to put some protein into you if this guy is going to get back up to speed," Gloria said, an hour or two later. She was sitting up, tenderly stroking his cock, while he luxuriated in one of those half-sleeping, half-waking moments that are common just before dawn.

"Sure you don't want to just to send down to the front desk for some Viagra?" he asked.

She laughed, but gently. "That's one expense I think we can hold off on, at least for now."

"Yeah—why help empower Bob Dole?"

"Well, are we going to call room service or not?"

"Sure. But first I have something I'd like to give you." He disappeared into the bathroom for a moment. When he returned, he was wheeling a mobile wine bucket filled with ice and the bottle of Mumm's.

Inside the white linen napkin he had placed over the champagne to keep it cold, he had taped the plain gold ring. "Let's see how it fits," he said. Slowly and tenderly, he put the ring onto her finger. To his great delight, the ring looked as if it had always been there.

"Now, don't you be going and gaining any weight so the ring loses its perfect fit," he said, after they'd toasted each other.

"Well, if *that* isn't the pot calling the kettle black," she laughed, giving him a playful poke in the left love handle. "But we don't have to start dieting today," she added, picking up the phone to call room service.

"Or any day!" he said, taking her in his arms and running his fingers teasingly over her breasts. "Or any day."

"Somehow I suspect you're right," she said, resignedly hanging up the phone to respond to her lover's caresses, which were starting to move toward her nether regions.

"Aren't I always?" he laughed. But although such a remark might at another time have drawn a saucy rejoinder or a smack on the butt from the spirited Gloria, by now she was too busy licking his cock and stroking his thighs to respond at all—other than by giving his cock a mostly playful nip. One with just enough sting to it to attract and keep his undivided attention.

Somehow, he never did get around to asking her what she thought the publisher would do if he gave the Staten Island reading a miss the next day—or why it had been booked for him in the first place. Whether that reading did in fact take place, I leave to your fertile imagination. But in closing, let me say that I have it on good authority the two remained at the Chuzzlewit for several days longer, necessitating some rearrangements in the reading tour which Gloria was more than happy to make on this occasion. I also know that they left the hotel only twice before finally checking out: once to buy some much-needed cranberry juice and more champagne and the second time to buy new tennis rackets. Advantage: mutual.

~ ᶠinis~

About the Author

JON PEIRCE grew up in the New York City suburb of Darien, Connecticut, where he learned to play tennis. He later attended Phillips Academy (Andover) and Amherst College, graduating from the latter in 1967 with a degree in English. After doing alternate service as a social worker for the Baltimore Welfare Department, he moved to Halifax in 1970 to do graduate work in English at Dalhousie University. Eventually he obtained an M.A. and Ph.D. in English from Dalhousie and taught English literature and composition for five years. But a shortage of jobs in the field caused him to make a career switch, to industrial relations, in which he received a master's degree from Queen's University. A succession of research and teaching jobs in industrial relations followed, as well as a stint doing doctoral work in the field at the University of Toronto. Finally, in 2001, he obtained a position with the Professional Institute of the Public Service of Canada, a union representing professionals in the federal public service. There he spent the last decade of his working life, working primarily as a labour relations officer.

A writer since boyhood, Jon began his free-lance career in 1981, publishing primarily in the *Kingston Whig-Standard* but also in such newspapers and magazines as *The Globe & Mail, Books in Canada, Ottawa Citizen, Christian Science Monitor,* and *Toronto Star.* He's the author of an industrial relations textbook and an essay collection. An actor as well as a writer, he has appeared in five community theatre productions across Metro Halifax and is preparing to appear in another with South Shore Players. He's also a playwright, with two one-act comedies and a full-length biopic to his credit. Outside of writing and theatre, his major interests include (surprise, surprise) tennis, cooking, swimming, bridge, civilized conversation, and progressive politics.